a minedition book
published by Penguin Young Readers Group

Compilation copyright © 2002 by Brigitte Weninger
Connecting stories text © 2002 by Brigitte Weninger
Cover art, endpapers, title page and connecting stories art © 2002 by Miriam Monnier
First American edition, 2004
Originally published in German in 2002 by Michael Neugebauer Verlag AG.

Published simultaneously in Canada.
Manufactured in Hong Kong by Wide World Ltd.
Designed by Michael Neugebauer
Typesetting in Veljovic, designed by Jovica Veljovic.
Color separation by Artwork, Laufen, Germany

Library of Congress Cataloging-in-Publication Data available upon request.

ISBN 0-698-40005-4
10 9 8 7 6 5 4 3 2 1
First Impression

For more information please visit our website: www.minedition.com

The Angel
and the Christmas Rabbit
and **24** Advent Stories
selected by Brigitte Weninger

Stories by:
Linard Bardill
Max Bolliger
Géraldine Elschner
Bruno Hächler
Charise Neugebauer
Konrad Richter
Karl Rühmann
Gerda Marie Scheidl
Leo Tolstoi
Brigitte Weninger

Translated by
Charise Myngheer and
Harold D. Morgan

Illustrations by:
Sonja Bougajeva
Alexandra Junge
Angela Kehlenbeck
Julie Litty
Anne Möller
Miriam Monnier
Birte Müller
Barbara Nascimbeni
Mirko Rathke
Lieselotte Schwarz
Elena Schern
Nina Spranger
Jochen Stuhrmann
Eve Tharlet

minedition

1 Ronnie Rabbit and the Carrot
a traditional folktale, picture by Birte Müller — 13

2 Lumina
Brigitte Weninger, picture by Julie Litty — 17

3 STINKY-TO-DIE-BORING!
Linard Bardill, picture by Miriam Monnier — 21

4 The Real Secret of the Stars
Karl Rühmann, picture by Mirko Rathke — 25

5 Martin the Shoemaker
Leo Tolstoy, picture by Mirko Rathke — 29

6 Santa Claus Is Coming
Konrad Richter, picture by Jochen Stuhrmann — 33

7 A Letter to Santa Claus
Brigitte Weninger, picture by Anne Möller — 37

8 Gregory, the Guardian Angel
Karl Rühmann, picture by Mirko Rathke — 41

9 The Gingerbread Man
a traditional folktale, picture by Birte Müller — 45

10 Anna's Wish
Bruno Hächler, picture by Nina Spranger — 49

11 Flowers for the Snowman
Gerda Marie Scheidl, picture by Elena Schern — 53

12 Pancakes for the Angel
Géraldine Elschner, picture by Alexandra Junge — 57

13 The Little Cookie Monster
Karl Rühmann, picture by Sonja Bougajeva — 61

14 Moonchild, Star of the Sea
Géraldine Elschner, picture by Lieselotte Schwarz — 65

15 The Christmas Flower
Géraldine Elschner, picture by Sonja Bougajeva — 69

16 Snow Ravens
Bruno Hächler, picture by Birte Müller — 73

17 Merry Christmas, Davy!
Brigitte Weninger, picture by Eve Tharlet — 77

18 A Winter Story
Max Bolliger, picture by Alexandra Junge — 81

19 A Doll for Jonathan
Brigitte Weninger, picture by Nina Spranger — 85

20 Santa's Gift
Charise Neugebauer, picture by Barbara Nascimbeni — 89

21 The Bears' Christmas Surprise
Bruno Hächler, picture by Angela Kehlenbeck — 93

22 Willard, The Little Christmas Tree
Karl Rühmann, picture by Anne Möller — 97

23 Silent Night
Brigitte Weninger, picture by Nina Spranger — 101

24 Story 24
Brigitte Weninger, picture by Miriam Monnier — 105

The sun was already setting as the old rabbit hopped across the meadow at the edge of the woods. He scratched the frozen ground looking for something to eat. The old rabbit nibbled on a wilted clump of clover here, then on a stalk there. The sky was flaming red from the setting sun. As he looked up, he thought about his grandmother. Once during Advent, she had told him a story about how angels in heaven bake cookies in huge ovens... Even though he wasn't really sure if it was true, the thought made him smile.

The old rabbit gazed across the meadow. He felt that something special was about to happen. As he perked up his ears to really listen, he heard a very fine ringing and singing in the air, "Hallelujah, hallelujah!"

"Holly-upsidaisy!"

Suddenly, right in front of the old rabbit's nose, a tousled little angel somersaulted into the grass. He was wearing a yellow cap with a pompom dangling from the top. Surprised, the old rabbit hopped back a few steps. "I'm sorry," apologized the little angel. "I didn't mean to do that—I'm not very good at landings." He pulled his cap back down over his ears and tried to rub a dirty spot from his clothes.

"Oh, my stars," grumbled the little angel unhappily. "Do you think it will come out if I spit on it?" he asked the rabbit.
The old rabbit shook his head. "Just let it dry and then you can brush it off."

"Okay, thanks," said the little angel politely. "Then I'll dry." And he plopped down next to the rabbit in the leaves.

"I don't think that's a good idea. You might catch a cold," said the rabbit concerned. But, the little one shook his head: "Angels don't catch colds." The little angel looked around the meadow with big wide eyes.

"Are you looking for something?" asked the old rabbit.

"Yes," answered the angel. "Actually, I'm looking for a present. But it's not a present for just anybody, so it has to be special. It has to be the present of presents!" The little angel bent a long rabbit ear towards him and whispered, "It's for..."

"Really?" said the old rabbit amazed. "And you're supposed to find this present here on earth?"

"Exactly," nodded the little angel proudly. "Every year one of us is allowed to fly off and search for something. This year, it's me. Can you imagine that?

Do you know of an extra-special present? It's kind of hard to find something new." The old rabbit folded his ears down over his eyes.

He found it easier to think that way. Suddenly, his expression changed and his ears went straight up again.

"A juicy carrot," he announced. "That would be a wonderful present."

"What? A carrot? That's a silly present," giggled the little angel.

"Why do you think a carrot is silly?" asked the old rabbit in an insulted tone. "I can't think of a better present than a carrot."

"That's because you're a rabbit," answered the little angel. "But not everybody likes carrots. When you're thinking about a present for someone, you have think about what would make THEM happy. And a carrot..."

10

The old rabbit interrupted him. "I'm certainly not the only one who would be happy with a fat juicy carrot! Don't you know the story about the little rabbit and the carrot?"

"No," said the little angel as his eyes lit up. "Please tell me, please tell me! I love stories."

"Okay, okay!" The old rabbit cleared his throat and then he told the first story.

RONNIE RABBIT AND THE CARROT

In the middle of winter, Ronnie Rabbit hopped across Farmer Brown's carrot field. He sniffed and dug around in the snow. He was hungry. Maybe I'll find an old carrot stalk to munch on! he thought.

Wow! He had great luck. Instead of a shriveled-up carrot stalk, he found two big, juicy carrots! Two! Happily, Ronnie Rabbit enjoyed the first carrot until it was all gone and he was stuffed. Now, what should I do with the second one? Hmmmm, it would be a shame to waste such a big, juicy carrot! thought Ronnie Rabbit. Then, he had a wonderful idea. I'll give it to my friend Danny Deer. I bet he's hungry!

Robbie Rabbit took the carrot to Danny Deer's hiding place. But no one was home. So Ronnie Rabbit left the carrot under the tree branches and happily hopped off.

When Danny Deer came home, he saw the carrot. He had just eaten a huge pile of hay in the forest and was stuffed. Hmmmm, it would be a shame to waste such a big, juicy carrot! thought Danny Deer. Then, he had a wonderful idea. I'll give it to my friend Willy Wild Boar. I bet he's hungry!

Danny Deer took the carrot to the cave where Willy Wild Boar usually slept. But no one was home. So Danny Deer left the carrot in the cooler and happily ran home.

When Willy Wild Boar came home, he saw the carrot. He had just come from Farmer Brown's orchard. He had eaten most of the apples that had fallen to the ground and he was stuffed. Hmmmm, it would be a shame to waste such a big, juicy carrot, thought Willy Wild Boar.

Then, he had a wonderful idea. I'll give it to my friend Otis Owl. I bet he's hungry!

Willy Wild Boar took the carrot to Otis Owl's tree hole, but he was sleeping. So Willy Wild Boar rolled the carrot inside and happily ran home. When Otis Owl woke up, he stretched and bumped the carrot. "Hey! What's that?" he said surprised. "Someone left a carrot for me? It was a nice gesture, but I would never be happy with a carrot. I don't like vegetables!"

Hmmmm, it would be terrible to waste such a big, juicy carrot! thought Otis Owl. Then he had a wonderful idea. I'll give it to my friend Ronnie Rabbit. I bet he's hungry!

Otis Owl took the carrot to Ronnie Rabbit's house, but no one was home. So Otis Owl left the carrot in front of the door and happily flew home.

When Ronnie Rabbit came home, he was cold, tired, and hungry. He saw the big, juicy carrot in front of his house. "Wow! Do I have luck!" he said.

"I'm hungry and it's as if this big, juicy carrot has fallen from heaven just for me.

And Ronnie Rabbit enjoyed the big, juicy carrot until it was all gone...and he was stuffed!

"Oh, my stars! That was a great story!" said the little angel in the yellow cap. "But, see, the owl didn't want the carrot as a present either!"

"You're right," said the old rabbit. He thought about it a little more as he looked at the lights in the distant city. "Could someone actually give light as a present?"

"Of course," answered the little angel, quite sure of himself. "That's what Lumina received once!"

The old rabbit perked up his ears and asked, "Who is Lumina?"

And the little angel told the second story.

LUMINA

Lumina had traveled a long distance. Her mother and father had passed away, and she was left alone. She had no home, she had no bed, and she had no food unless someone was kind and gave her something to eat.

The only thing that Lumina owned was a little lantern that her mother had given her. Lumina loved her lantern and took good care of it. It provided light when it was dark and warmth when it was cold.

Lumina wandered through the countryside. She was never able to stay anywhere for long, because people chased her from their doorsteps, saying, "Go away, little beggar girl!"

After being chased off one evening, Lumina went into the forest to look for a place to sleep. An icy wind blew through the branches, nipping Lumina's cheeks and causing the light in her lantern to flicker. She tried to shelter the flame with her coat, but a gust of wind blew and her light went out. It was very dark in the forest. It was very cold. Lumina began to cry.

When she dried her tears and lifted her head, she saw a faint glow in the trees above her. The glow came from an old owl. "Oh owl, if only you could help me," Lumina said softly. The owl flew out of the tree and settled on the ground at Lumina's feet. Then he flew from the ground and came down again a little farther in front of her. Lumina realized he wanted her to follow him!

The old owl led Lumina through the forest. At last they reached a wide road.

"Thank you for your help, dear owl!" she said. "I can find my own way now." The owl brushed Lumina's hand with his wing and flew away.

Suddenly Lumina saw two lights in the distance! A horse-drawn sleigh was racing down the road. Lumina shouted and waved, but the sleigh just drove past. She dropped her arms feeling very sad and alone. She tried to think about what she should do. Lumina decided to stay on the road, so that she wouldn't get lost.

Leaning into the wind, Lumina went on along the dark road. Then she saw another light! There was a boy carrying a lantern. Lumina was so happy she ran to meet the boy. But when he heard her footsteps, he stopped in alarm.

"Don't be frightened!" shouted Lumina. "I only want to ask for your help— I need your lantern!"

The boy shone his lantern into Lumina's face.

"I'm sorry," he said, "but I can't give you my lantern. If I gave you my lantern I wouldn't be able to find my way home."

"No, no," Lumina said. "I have a lantern of my own. I only want you to light it again."

"Oh, I can do that," said the boy. Very carefully he took the flaming wick out of his lantern and held it against the wick of Lumina's. Soon both lanterns were burning with strong, steady flames. A warm glow came into Lumina's face.

"Thank you!" she said. The boy looked down at his own lantern. It seemed to be shining more brightly now.

"You'd better come back to our farm with me," said the boy. "You shouldn't be outdoors in such cold weather." Their lanterns showed them the way and Lumina followed the boy home.

The boy's family welcomed Lumina and shared their simple Christmas Eve supper with her. They invited her to stay and by the time spring arrived, Lumina had become a part of their family. Every evening that Lumina lit her lantern, she was thankful for her new home.

18

"Very nice," nodded the old rabbit, looking satisfied. "It's good to have a home and friends. Being alone is really awful."

"Exactly," agreed the little angel. "And on top of it, it's stinky-to-die boring!"

The old rabbit looked at him curiously. "Do you know the story about Repeat Rabbit?"

"No, I don't," admitted the little angel, moving a bit closer. "Tell me! Tell me! Why is he called Repeat Rabbit?"

And the old rabbit told the third story.

STINKY-TO-DIE-BORING!

Repeat Rabbit's real name is Ronald, but everybody calls him Repeat. They call him Repeat because he says everything twice.

One day Repeat was bored. The day was just dragging on!

Repeat's best friend, Bernie Bear, was in hibernation. His other friend, Donnie Deer, was writing a story and Repeat didn't think there could be anything more boring than that.

"It's all so STINKY-TO-DIE-BORING!" shouted Repeat looking high up into the sky.

Then he stopped and thought about it. Is dying really boring?

If not, then he could play dead. At least that way he would have something to do.

And that's just what he did. Repeat climbed up into a tree, pulled his body over a branch, and let his legs and head hang down...and he pretended to be dead.

Then a snowbird flew by and saw Repeat hanging there and asked, "What are you doing?"

"I'm playing dead, playing dead," answered Repeat.

"Why?" asked the snowbird.

"Because I'm waiting, I'm waiting," said Repeat.

"What are you waiting for?" asked the snowbird.

"For something to happen," answered Repeat.

"Interesting," said the snowbird.

She landed on the branch beside Repeat. "Just hang down?" she asked.

"Yeah, just hang. Hang down."

The bird held on tightly to the branch, leaned backwards and hung upside down next to Repeat...just like a bat ... and pretended to be dead.

Then a wild boar came along, saw the two of them and asked, "What are you two doing?"

"We're playing dead," answered the snowbird.

And the wild boar asked, "What's it like?"

"It's just like when you hang upside-down, you hang upside-down," explained Repeat.

And the snowbird nagged, "Try it yourself and stop asking dumb questions!"

So the wild boar climbed up and wrapped his tail around the branch. He let himself fall and he pretended to be dead.

A short time later, the wild boar decided that dying was a little boring. "Wouldn't we rather play cards?" he asked.

The snowbird felt that dying was more interesting than playing cards and said, "We were here first!"

But Repeat interrupted them both and said, "First we are playing a round of dying. Afterwards we can still play cards, play cards!"

"CRACK! SNAP!" The branch suddenly cracked and broke, and all three of them flipped over and landed in the snow! Repeat shook the snow from his ears and said with a smile, "I had no idea that dying could be so dangerous!"

The wild boar flipped back over and asked, "Are we going to play cards now or not?"

"Only if I get to go first," chirped the snowbird. So they all went to Repeat's hole and drank juice. Then Repeat shuffled the cards, the wild boar munched on a bag of nuts, and the snowbird sang her favorite song while they played cards. They played and played and played.

...And if they haven't died, they're still playing.

"Wow! That was another great story," said the little angel and the pompom on his cap bounced as he laughed.

"That's a terrific cap," admired the old rabbit. "Do all angels wear them?"

"No, only the ones that travel a lot to look after the new stars... and I'm one of them," admitted the little angel proudly.

"Really?" said the old rabbit. "I've often wondered what stars are made of. Would you tell me something about them?"

And the little angel told the fourth story.

THE REAL SECRET OF THE STARS

On a beautiful clear night, a young boy and his grandfather crossed a field. The young boy enjoyed spending time with his grandfather. He knew many great stories and the little boy felt like his grandfather could pick stories the way most other people picked flowers. Both of them stood still and looked up into the sky. "Isn't it wonderful?" said his grandfather. "It's as though the stars are sending us secret messages when they blink."

"Grandfather," said the young boy. "Where do stars come from anyway?"

"Well I've heard a few stories," he answered. "For example, the one about the sea robber."

"Oh please, I want to hear it!" shouted the young boy excitedly. And his grandfather began telling him the story:

Once upon a time, a long, long time ago, there lived a daring and frightful sea robber. He robbed huge merchant ships and took their jewels, pearls, silver, and gold. He was good at stealing and very brave. But as time went on, he became more and more greedy. Just once he wanted to steal a huge sack of gold nuggets to add to his stash of treasures. But when he did, his sack was so full that the nuggets spilled out and rolled across the sky.

"The stars in the sky are gold nuggets? Wow!" said the young boy amazed.

"Well, maybe they're something else," grinned grandfather. "Once upon a time there was a magician. He could perform such wonderful magic that everyone had heard of him. One night he decided to try to fill his hut with shining stars. He was able to do it. And it was beautiful. After he had fallen asleep, a bat saw the lights and flew into the hut. The bat accidentally tickled the magician on the nose. He was terribly frightened so he opened the door of his hut and ran out. And you can imagine what happened! The stars fell out and scattered themselves all over the sky."

The young boy laughed. "That must have made the magician angry!"

But his grandfather didn't answer, because he knew another story.

"Somewhere I heard that the sky's underside is really a huge cooking pot! Can you imagine? Inside this pot they cook the light for an entire day! And this light must be stirred constantly so that it doesn't burn. Over time, when it's not stirred enough, the bottom of the pot gets small holes. They say that the stars are just the light shining through the small holes!"

The young boy looked up at the sky with fascination and imagined some one with a huge spoon stirring light.

"Then the moon is also a hole in the bottom of the pot—but a much bigger one!" he said thoughtfully.

Then the grandfather picked up the young boy and lifted him high into the air so that he was closer to the stars and whispered in his ear, "Those were just stories. Now I will tell you the real secret about the stars." The young boy listened with anticipation.

"Every star that you see is a child's wish. Whenever a child wishes for something, a new star appears in the sky. That particular star will stay in the sky until the perfect time for that child's wish to come true.

So whenever you look up at the sky, you should think about all of your wishes. One day each one will come true. And then you'll see a wonderful falling star cross the sky!"

"That's beautiful," whispered the young boy. "Grandfather, could I make a wish right now?"

"Of course," laughed grandfather. "The more wishes you make, the brighter the sky will be!"

The young boy put his cheek to his grandfather's face and wished for something wonderful...

And together they searched for the new star.

26

The old rabbit and the little angel sat staring thoughtfully at the sky full of beautiful stars.

Finally the old rabbit whispered, "So that's the secret about the stars."

The little angel nodded and smiled. "It must be a wonderful feeling when an important wish comes true," he continued. "Just like the time with Martin the shoemaker who lives in the city."

"What was his wish?" asked the little angel nosily.

And the old rabbit told the fifth story.

MARTIN THE SHOEMAKER

Martin the shoemaker lived and worked in an old basement in a small town. Through his window he could only see the feet of the people who passed by. That was how he recognized everyone. Martin worked as long as there was daylight. In the evening he fixed himself a cup of tea, took his Bible from his bookshelf, and read. This always made Martin feel good. As he finished his reading, he thought to himself longingly, Oh, how nice it would be to have met Jesus. Then a quiet voice said his name.

"Martin! Look outside your window tomorrow morning and I will come and visit you!" Shocked, Martin looked around the room, but no one was there. Martin shook his head a little confused and then fell asleep.

The next morning when Martin was cutting his leather, he heard foot-steps in front of the window. He recognized the huge boots of Stephen, the old street sweeper. Stephen stomped his feet and blew warm air into his cold hands. Martin opened the basement window and yelled, "Come on in!" The street sweeper sat down by the heater and Martin offered him a cup of tea. "Thank you. Now I'm warm again," Stephen said with a smile. And he went back to work.

At lunchtime, Martin fixed a pot of soup. As he looked out the window he saw a young woman carrying a small child. She was trying to protect the child from the cold wind with her thin dress. Martin called to her and invited her inside. He offered her a bowl of soup and gave her his old coat.

"Thank you for everything," the woman said with a smile. She wrapped the child in the warm coat and left.

Martin went back to his work. He heard a loud voice and looked up. A woman from the market was scolding a young boy for stealing one of her apples. She yelled at the boy and shook him until Martin stood between them. "Please let him go! What he did wasn't right, but don't we all make mistakes?"

"I'm really sorry," said the young boy. Then he took the woman's basket from her arms and carried it to the market for her.

It began to get dark, so Martin lit his lamp and finished sewing the boots he had been working on.

Then he sat at his table and began to read his Bible. Suddenly, Martin heard a voice whisper quietly in his ear. "Martin, I was with you today. Did you recognize me?"

"What? When?" asked Martin looking uncertain.

Then in the glow from the lamp, Martin saw Stephen the old street sweeper, the young mother with her child, and the old woman from the market. They were all smiling at him.

They appeared in a mist before his eyes and then they disappeared just as quickly. For the first time Martin realized that the night before had not been a dream. Today Jesus had really visited him. The shoemaker was full of joy. Martin continued to read the story in the Bible and it said what Jesus had said many years before, "What you have done for my poorest brother, you have done for me."

"Do you think that shoes or boots would be the right gift?" asked the little angel, thinking it over and looking down at his own bare feet.

"I really don't know," answered the old rabbit, sounding a bit doubtful. "Didn't you want something really, really special?"

"Of course!" complained the little angel. "But I can't think of anything." The little angel smiled. "But I can think of a story about boots. Do you want to hear it?"

The old rabbit nodded and the little angel told the sixth story.

SANTA CLAUS IS COMING

Early that morning Stevie had gone into the forest with his uncle to feed the animals. When he got home, he entered the house like a whirlwind and ran straight into the kitchen. "Mom, Mom! I have to tell you something! You won't believe what happened..."

"First you have to take off your boots!" his mother interrupted. "How many times do I have to tell you to take your boots off before coming into the house?"

"I know. I know," grumbled Stevie. Disappointed, he turned around and carefully tiptoed back out of the house. Stevie lost all interest in telling his mother what had happened.

Unhappily, he walked towards the shed in the back yard. Stevie had promised to help his uncle load the wagon with hay and get it ready for the next day.

"Why do you look so sad?" asked his uncle. "Aren't you excited? Santa Claus is coming!"

"Oh no!" Stevie said. He had been so busy helping his uncle, he had completely forgotten. Suddenly his face looked even worse when he realized that Santa might know about the incident with his dirty boots. Stevie felt miserable. He stomped off and shouted, "I think Santa Claus is stupid! And he can just keep his Christmas presents!"

Stevie's stomach began to ache. He ran to the back door and sat down on the stairs. He knew he was making things worse for himself. What if Santa had heard what he said about him?

Stevie's mother called for him, "Stevie, come inside. I have a surprise for you!" As Stevie walked inside, there was a loud knock at the front door. A tall man in a red coat and a long white beard entered the room. It was Santa Claus. The farther Santa came into the room, the farther back into the corner Stevie crouched—until he was sitting on the floor under the table. All Stevie could see were Santa's big, black boots.

As he watched, Stevie couldn't believe it. Snow from Santa's boots was falling on the floor and melting. He immediately came out from under the table.

"Look, Mom. Santa has dirty boots on, too!" Speechless, Santa and Stevie's mother stared at the dirty boots and the puddle on the floor. Suddenly Santa started to laugh and Stevie's mother laughed, too.

Santa sat down on a nearby stool and looked at Stevie "Even Santa can make a mistake. Should we both make a promise to your mother that we won't come into the house with dirty shoes anymore?" Stevie nodded yes as he made the promise with Santa.

They talked for a long time. Santa was proud of Stevie, because he had been helping his uncle and tending to the animals. When Stevie went to bed he was very happy. He knew that Santa would leave him a wonderful surprise. That night he dreamed about the animals, the forest, and his good friend Santa Claus!

"I know you know who Santa Claus is," smiled the old rabbit. "But there is another man with a white beard, who put on a red coat and delivered a big bag full of presents. Do you know who he is?"

"No," the little angel answered. "Is he one of Santa's friends?"

"Of course!" said the rabbit. "Once there was a little boy who was very good, but he didn't know about Santa Claus and wishes".

And the old rabbit told the seventh story.

A LETTER TO SANTA CLAUS

Oliver and his mother lived in a small village high up in the mountains. They were very poor. Oliver's mother was a seamstress, but there wasn't much work for her. Every day after school Oliver gathered firewood from the hills to sell in the village, but even so, they only had enough money for bare necessities.

One evening when the baker's wife came to pick up her new dress, she gave Oliver an old calendar with colorful pictures. Underneath the picture for December it read, "Every year Santa Claus comes from the North Pole on his sleigh pulled by reindeer and brings gifts for all good children."

This surprised Oliver. He had never received a gift from Santa. Wasn't he good enough? Or was it because he had never wished for anything? How would Santa even know that he existed? Sadly, Oliver pulled the blanket over his head and fell asleep. The next day, Oliver ran into his friend Jacob the mailman.

"I brought you a present," whispered Jacob. It was a big red balloon! Oliver was so happy he could barely speak.

The balloon was beautiful. It was as red as Santa Claus's coat and as round as his belly. It bounced around playfully in the wind! As Oliver watched the balloon, he had an idea. "If I let go of the string, the balloon will fly up into the clouds...maybe as far as the North Pole!" Oliver's heart suddenly beat faster. He ran home, tore a sheet of paper from his notebook, and wrote a letter to Santa Claus. In his letter he wished for a pair of warm boots and thick gloves for winter and a lamp for his mother so she could sew in the evening.

Oliver attached the letter to the string of the balloon. Then he climbed to the top of the mountain above the village. He looked into the distance for a long time. Where was the North Pole? Should he really let such a wonderful balloon fly away? But it was the only chance he had to reach Santa Claus.

Oliver checked the knot on the string once more. Then he gave the balloon's fat cheek one last kiss and let it go. Unfortunately, the cold mountain wind wasn't blowing north. Instead it carried Oliver's Christmas balloon to the south, over forests, mountains, and valleys all the way to the sea. There, on the outskirts of a big city, the balloon was too weak to fly any farther. It bumped over the roof of a house and sank to the garden below...just as old Christopher trudged out of his house.

"What's this rubbish!" he grumbled. He read Oliver's letter. "Wishes for Santa Claus!" the old man snorted.

"Ha! The things these spoiled brats believe in. Ha! I used to have wishes, too." Christopher crumpled up the letter and threw it away.

But Christopher didn't sleep well that night. He couldn't stop thinking about Santa Claus and all the things he had wished for years ago...children and grandchildren... and now he was all alone. And this Oliver, maybe he wasn't such a spoiled brat after all—what kind of child wished for those sorts of things from Santa Claus?

At dawn, Christopher got up and pulled Oliver's letter out of the garbage. Two days later a strange man arrived at Oliver's village. He wore a red coat and had a bag full of packages with him. Above his head danced a red balloon.

Soon there was a knock at Oliver's door. And then Santa Claus entered the room. He brought fur-lined boots and nice warm mittens for Oliver. He brought a bright lamp and a soft shawl for Oliver's mother. He had apples and candy. And he also brought back the wonderful Christmas balloon, which he had refilled with air!

Santa Claus spent the whole evening at Oliver's house. He held Oliver's hand until he fell asleep, and afterward he talked to Oliver's mother for a long time.

In the morning, they loaded a bundle of clothes, the new lamp, and the sewing basket into a carriage and drove to the station.

Oliver and his mother live with Christopher now. They call him Grandfather. Every day after school Oliver plays in the garden, and old Christopher is happy again.

Every year at Christmas, Oliver, his mother, and Christopher buy a bright red balloon. They write Santa Claus a thank-you note, tie it to the balloon's string, and let the balloon fly over valleys, mountains, and forests all the way to the North Pole.

"Hey, a great big balloon like that would make a nice gift!" said the little angel when he remembered why he was here.

"That's true, but I'm afraid it wouldn't last very long," said the old rabbit.

"That's also true," sighed the little angel. "How did the others ever find their presents? Such a dumb silly thing! I should have asked my friend Gregory before I left. He is a really cool guardian angel and knows his way around earth."

The old rabbit was curious and asked, "How does one get to be a really cool guardian angel?"

And the little angel told the eighth story.

40

GREGORY, THE GUARDIAN ANGEL

One day Gregory sat daydreaming on his comfortable pink cloud. It was Sunday and nobody was doing anything foolish. As Gregory dangled his legs over the side of the cloud, a well-known voice called his name. Against his will, Gregory flipped over and floated off to take a look. A protection order! Oh no, not today, he thought. If he hadn't been an angel, he would have ignored it.

A large cloud finger pointed down to earth. "Do you see the little boy over there next to the wall? His name is Calvin. Today you are his guardian angel, so please look after him."

Gregory looked at the little boy. His baseball cap was on backwards, he had a band-aid on his elbow, and a bruised knee. He looks like he could use a guardian angel, thought Gregory. "Well, I guess I'll get started then," he sighed, and swooped down.

Gregory preferred to view earth from his cloud. But an order is an order and there was nothing he could do about it.

Calvin stood on the wall and got ready to jump down. "No!" shouted Gregory, forgetting that angels have to whisper if they want children to hear them.

"No!" he whispered as quickly as he could. But he was too late. The little boy jumped. Gregory was able to catch him, but they both somersaulted across the grass.

"This would have never happened on my cloud," grumbled the angel.

As Gregory sat up, he saw a butterfly on a flower. It's so beautiful the way the sun glistens on its colorful wings, thought Gregory, amazed. He would have never seen that from his cloud.

Suddenly, Gregory flew higher. He swooped here and there in excitement. Then he remembered Calvin. Where did he go?

Calvin stood in a flat pool and skipped stones across the water. "Well cloudburst and straight to earth," complained Gregory. "What does he think he's doing?" But, as he watched a little longer, he began to think skipping stones looked like a lot of fun. Gregory wanted to try it himself.

Unfortunately, angels can't hold stones. So as Calvin threw the next one, Gregory put his hand in Calvin's and they threw it together. "One, two… seven! Yippee!" they both cheered. What a great throw! Gregory wanted to do it again, but Calvin had already found something else to do.

"Oh, no. Does it have to be like this?" Gregory groaned as he watched Calvin cross the water over the large stones. Calvin bent down to the water. Gregory did, too. He was surprised at all the things he saw swimming in the flat pool. There were funny tadpoles and fast water bugs. He even saw a beautiful green frog. Calvin and Gregory bent farther down to get a closer look. Then the stone tipped and with one long movement, they had to jump to the water's edge.

Gregory was relieved that they didn't get very wet, but before he could relax, Calvin already had another idea. He was headed for the tree house! Skillfully, Calvin held on to the ladder and climbed up. Gregory didn't even have to help. He looked around excitedly. "I would love to have a leaf roof like this over my cloud!" thought Gregory. Calvin whistled with the birds and practiced spitting cherry seeds.

Later the two of them sat in front of a box where little men were jumping around inside and doing funny things. "This is fascinating, even for a guardian angel," thought Gregory. But when he realized it wasn't real, he laughed at himself.

Before long it was time to go to bed. Calvin was tucked in and Gregory needed to return home. He looked over his shoulder and took one last look at Calvin's room before he left. As he saw the bookcase full of beautiful books, he sighed. "Wow! I would love to have a funny box and a book shelf like Calvin's on my cloud."

It was already dark when Gregory got home. He made himself comfortable on his soft pink cloud and stretched his wings.

"So how was your day on earth? Stressful?" asked the great voice from the big white cloud.

"You know, it was actually pretty cool! I'll definitely visit again!" Gregory smiled a great big smile, pulled his baseball cap down over his face, and fell asleep.

"Yes, sometimes even angels can learn something new!" laughed the old rabbit.
"Would you ever want to become a guardian angel for children?"

"Of course, but first I have to learn how to land better," admitted the little angel, and he blushed red all the way up to his pompom. "I can't catch very well, either. Sometimes I practice with little stars that whiz around. But I think children are faster."

"If you keep practicing, you'll be able to do it someday," consoled the old rabbit. "There are some who can't even catch a gingerbread man..."

And the old rabbit told the ninth story.

THE GINGERBREAD MAN

Once upon a time there was a woman who loved to bake. One day, shortly before Christmas, she made a large gingerbread man.

Two juicy raisins were his eyes, a red candy cherry was his nose, and white sliced almonds formed his mouth.

Proudly she laid the gingerbread man on the cookie sheet and put it into the oven. Immediately, she heard a rumble and knocking from inside. A small voice shouted, "Let me out! Let me out!"

The old woman ran to the oven and opened the door.

The gingerbread man jumped up and ran away.

"Wait! Stay here!" the old woman shouted as she ran after him.

But the gingerbread man looked at the woman and sang,

"Run, run as fast as you can.
You can't catch me, I'm the gingerbread man!"

And tiddle-di-dum—he kept running and left the old woman shouting.

The gingerbread man met a cat in the yard. The cat's eyes got big and hungry when she saw him. "Wait! Stay here!" she meowed as she ran after him.

But the gingerbread man just looked at the cat and sang,

"Run, run as fast as you can.
You can't catch me, I'm the gingerbread man!"

And tiddle-di-dum—he kept running and let the old woman shout and the cat meow.

The gingerbread man met a dog by the fence. The dog's mouth watered when he saw him. "Wait! Stay here!" he barked as he ran after him.

But the gingerbread man just looked at the dog and sang,

"Run, run as fast as you can.
You can't catch me, I'm the gingerbread man!"

And tiddle-di-dum—he kept running and let the old woman shout, the cat meow, and the dog bark.

The gingerbread man met a sheep on the snow-covered hill. The sheep shook its head at such a sight. "Wait! Stay here!" bleated the sheep as he ran after him.

But the gingerbread man just looked at the sheep and sang,

"Run, run as fast as you can.
You can't catch me, I'm the gingerbread man!"

And tiddle-di-dum—he kept running and let the old woman shout, the cat meow, the dog bark, and the sheep bleat!

The gingerbread man met a fox in the woods. The fox smacked his lips at such a delicious sight.

"Wait! Stay here!" howled the fox as he ran after him.

But the gingerbread man just looked at the fox and sang,

"Run, run as fast as you can.
You can't catch me, I'm the gingerbread man!"

And tiddle-di-dum—he kept running and let the old woman shout, the cat meow, the dog bark, the sheep bleat, and the fox howl!

The gingerbread man met two little children in the middle of the road. They were all alone. They waved to him. "Please, please sweet gingerbread man. Wait! Stay here! We are soooooo hungry!"

And tiddle-di-dee—the gingerbread man stopped running. He jumped high in the air and landed in their basket. The gingerbread man couldn't imagine anything better than to be eaten by two hungry children.

"Yummm! Gingerbread tastes soooo good!" said the little angel, rubbing his tummy.

"I like it, too!" agreed the old rabbit, "although I think I would like a juicy carrot better."

"Stop with your silly carrot!" said the little angel. "I'd rather smell gingerbread!"

"And I smell snow," said the old rabbit, with his nose positioned high in the air.

"Snow—that would be lovely!" said the little angel. "Little Anna also wished for snow..."

And the little angel told the tenth story.

ANNA'S WISH

It hadn't snowed in Anna's town for many years. When the last leaves disappeared from the trees and the stormy fall wind turned into a cold whisper, fog covered the city like a gray towel. Over time people's faces began to look as gray as the weather.

But one day something strange happened. Anna was walking through town with her mother. As she stood in front of the bakery window, she suddenly felt something she couldn't explain. Something fine and cool touched her cheeks. But nothing was there.

A week later, when she and her mother were walking past the bakery, it happened again. Something touched her cheeks so lightly that it felt like a kiss from a butterfly. Anna stopped and looked around. At first she thought that the kids from school were playing a trick on her. But no one else was there.

The bakery window was decorated for Christmas. It looked like a real winter landscape. There was even a snow-white pony made of wood. His mane looked like packed bristles. Unfortunately, one of his wooden legs was broken. But his eyes sparkled as bright as winter stars.

"Mom, what is snow like?" she asked out of the blue.

It had been a long time since her mother had seen snow. She must have been a little girl about Anna's age then.

"Snow is white and cold," answered her mother.

"What else?"

"Snow flakes look like stars. No two of them are the same. Some of them are like air. Others are thick and sticky. If you catch one on your tongue, it melts like strawberry ice cream."

"Tell me more!" begged Anna.

"Oh, snow is wonderful!" her mother said as her face began to glow. "We used to play outside after lunch. We built fat snowmen with round stomachs and carrot noses. We threw snowballs and hid in snow forts. When it was really cold and the pond froze, we went ice-skating. That was really fun!"

They were both quiet for a while. Then Anna said, "If only it would snow again..."

That night, Anna dreamed that she was a snowflake.

First thing the next morning, she ran to the window. But there was no snow.

Anna was disappointed. She ran to the bakery. The small wooden pony was still in the window. He looked as if he had been waiting for her. She stood there for a long time looking into his bright eyes. As she watched him, she wished that it would snow. She wished and wished—over and over again. She had never wished for anything so hard in her whole life.

Small stars immediately swooped Anna's wishes up and carried them high into the sky where they were frozen into ice crystals. And then softly they fell back down again—as snowflakes. At first there were just a few. Then there were more and more. Hundreds. Thousands. There were hundreds of thousands. Anna had stopped attempting to count them all. They fell down everywhere—all over the city. They covered the houses, the streets, the trees, and the bushes. It wasn't long before you could hear the sound of shovels outside doorways. People's faces were no longer gray. Everyone was happy. They were smiling. Finally the snowflakes slowed down. Anna felt exhausted. She looked inside the bakery window again, but the wooden pony was gone.

Anna pulled her cap down over her ears and went straight home to build a snowman.

As she walked down the snow-covered street, she felt something fine and cool touch her cheeks. She couldn't explain it, but as she looked around, she smiled.

"You're right," admitted the old rabbit. "It's beautiful when it snows. Unfortunately, it makes searching for food more difficult. But the flowers sleep better during winter under a blanket of snow. And in spring, the clover grows even juicier, and the carrots..."

"Oh, my stars!" yelped the little angel. "I can't hear another word about you and your carrots! I would prefer to hear that you've built a snowman."

"Sorry," answered the old rabbit. "I've never built a snowman. But I did meet one once."

"How strange," the little angel said.

And the old rabbit told the eleventh story.

FLOWERS FOR THE SNOWMAN

In the middle of an open field there stood a large snowman with black coal eyes, a carrot nose, stick arms, and mittens. As far as he could see was white. The snowman looked thoroughly miserable. He had heard that there were flowers in all the colors of the rainbow. "But where were they?" he wondered. "Maybe I'm just standing in the wrong place. The flowers must be somewhere else," he thought to himself.

So the next morning the snowman set off to find the colorful flowers. On his way, he met a rabbit nibbling a cabbage stalk.

"Is that a flower?" asked the snowman.

"No," answered the rabbit. "It's a cabbage stalk."

"Well, where will I find flowers, flowers in all the colors of the rainbow?"

"You won't. Since you are made of winter snow, you'll never see the flowers grow!" mumbled the rabbit and he hopped away.

"Of course I will!" said the snowman. He plodded on until he came to a forest. All the trees were covered in a thick layer of snow. Only one small tree was showing its usual coat of green needles. It was crouching under the branches of a bigger fir tree.

"Is this a flower?" The snowman asked a crow that he saw nearby.

"No," croaked the crow. "It's a fir tree."

"Well, where will I find flowers, flowers in all the colors of the rainbow?"

"You won't. Since you are made of winter snow, you'll never see the flowers grow!" cawed the crow, and it flew away.

The snowman plodded on again. It was already dark when he came to a town.

"Hello, is anyone there?" called the snowman. But no one answered. Everyone was asleep. The snowman searched around, but he didn't find flowers anywhere.

"Is this a flower?" he asked a cat who was sitting on a streetlamp.

"No!" meowed the cat. "It's a streetlamp!"

"Well, where can I find flowers, flowers in all the colors of the rainbow?"

"You won't. Since you are made of winter snow, you'll never see the flowers grow!" meowed the cat, and it scampered away.

Would he never get to see flowers because he was made of snow? The snowman felt sad and tired. He trudged across a courtyard. "Aah, I can rest here for a while," he yawned, as he leaned against a door.

The snowman shouldn't have done that. The door gave way, and he tumbled head over heels down a flight of stairs. Oh, dear! The snowman looked around anxiously. He saw all the colors of the rainbow. They must be flowers! he said to himself.

The snowman had stumbled into the greenhouse at a garden center. It was warm inside to protect the flowers from the frost.

"At last I have found flowers!" cried the snowman. "They make my heart glow with joy, but oh, I feel so weak." He sighed wearily, shutting his coal-black eyes and falling asleep.

The next morning, the head gardener found him. "This looks as if it was once a snowman. Out you go! This is no place for someone made of snow." And he shoveled what was left of the snowman into the yard.

"Poor snowman!" cried the children. "Let's make a new one."

The children made three snowballs and piled them on top of one another. They stuck on the carrot nose, the coal-black eyes, and the stick arms. They even put the mittens on!

"Hooray!" they shouted when they had finished.

And the snowman didn't look miserable at all. He was smiling. He was remembering the flowers, flowers in all the colors of the rainbow.

"Wow! I'm happy that everything turned out okay," said the little angel as he excitedly twirled the pompom on his hat. "I was afraid the snowman was gone for good."

"No, he was just gone for a little while," explained the rabbit. "And of course my favorite part was that he even got his carrot nose back!" he said as his eyes twinkled.

"I also know a story about something that disappeared for a while," the little angel interrupted. "But it wasn't a carrot. It was a pancake."

And the little angel told the twelfth story.

PANCAKES FOR THE ANGEL

Every Friday afternoon at Grandpa's was pancake day. It was his thirteen grandchildren's favorite day, and anyone who wanted to eat pancakes was invited. It was just that simple at Grandpa's house.

Over time, Grandpa became known as the Pancake King. He knew the recipe by heart and could find the ingredients with his eyes closed. He was able to flip them in the air as if he had been hired by the circus to perform just so.

"Fantastic!" applauded the children each week excitedly.

But one week something very strange happened.

It was a Friday in December. It was ice-cold and already dark outside when the children finally arrived. All thirteen grandchildren showed up and they all had red noses from the cold.

Grandfather had the children sit next to the fire to warm up while he began cooking in the kitchen. One pancake after the next: two, three, ten, twenty, twenty-six... Eventually, his arm began to hurt and the little kitchen became so warm that he decided to open the window. And then it happened...

Grandpa poured fresh batter into the pan.

The batter formed another perfect pancake. He waited a little and then threw the twenty-seventh pancake high into the air, and just like magic it disappeared.

Grandpa looked all around. He was confused. He looked up, but it wasn't stuck to the ceiling. He looked all around. It wasn't on the cabinet. And it wasn't on the floor. This just can't be, thought Grandpa.

"Grandpa, are they ready yet?" asked a small hungry voice. The whole group of children was standing there.

"Yes—I mean no," stuttered Grandpa. "My last pancake just disappeared!"

"Disappeared? How so?"

"I don't know!" he answered. "I threw it up into the air, just like I always do...and it never came down!"

"Probably a bad landing," decided Andy. "Or could it have flown away?"

"It doesn't matter! Can we just look for it," shouted Alice. "I'm hungry!"

And so everyone searched for it. They looked in every corner. But, it wasn't there. "Oh, my," sighed Grandfather and he went to the window to get some fresh air. And then he began to laugh out loud. "Come here children. Quick! I found it!"

Grandpa pointed up into the sky. And there it was—really! It was hanging between the stars, just a little to the right of the church tower.

"But Grandpa, that's the moon," said sweet little Mia.

Grandpa cleared his throat and said, "The moon? Not possible. Something that yellow and crispy can only be my pancake!"

"How are we suppose to get it back?" asked Tina.

"I can climb up on your shoulders," offered Leo.

"No, it's better if I get the ladder," said Paul.

"Maybe use a butterfly," suggested Marie.

"No way. A rocket!" shouted Lewis.

Grandpa wiped his brow. "No, children. Those ideas are a little too dangerous.

"You know what. We're going to eat our twenty-six pancakes in peace. And we're going to give the one up there to the angels."

"Yeah!" All the children agreed. They all sat at the table and enjoyed their pancakes.

The next morning, they knew that the angels had enjoyed theirs too, because there wasn't a pancake to be found in the sky!

The old rabbit and the little angel stared up at the moon. It shimmered through the clouds—full and round.

"It really does look like a pancake, doesn't it?" said the old rabbit.

"Or like a yellow Christmas cookie," added the little angel.

"Woooooo! The moon better look out for the cookie monster," mumbled the old rabbit in a deep voice.

The little angel looked at him surprise. "Who is the cookie monster? Should I be afraid of him?"

"No, only Christmas cookies need to be afraid of the cookie monster!"

And the old rabbit told the thirteenth story.

THE LITTLE COOKIE MONSTER

Mom had baked some delicious Christmas cookies: cinnamon stars, coconut macaroons, and almond cookies . They were in a cookie jar that looked like a treasure chest. Mom put the chest in a good hiding place that was suitable for a real treasure—in the very back of the closet. Nobody will find it there, she thought...nobody!

Then one night heavy footsteps could be heard. Bumm, bumm-bumm. The closet door creaked creepily.

Two long, blue-and-white-striped arms dove deep into the darkness of the closet. Two big hands found the jar, opened it, and took out some cinnamon stars. Then the jar was put back in its secret hiding place.

Early next morning the steps were heard again. Tapp-tapp-tapp. The closet door creaked creepily.

A fuzzy-haired head with dark curls spied around the clothes. Two hands found the small chest and took out a few coconut macaroons. Then the jar was put back in its secret hiding place.

About lunchtime footsteps flitted again. Tipp-tipp-tipp. The closet door creaked creepily.

A green body with a red design crept between the clothes. Two hands found the sweet-smelling treasure chest and grabbed a few almond cookies. Then the jar was put back in its secret hiding place.

Cookies continued to disappear in a very mysterious way.

One Sunday Mom decided to share some Christmas cookies with everyone. She pulled the jar out of its secret hiding place and opened it.

"That just can't be!" Mom yelled in astonishment. "What happened to my Christmas cookies? The jar is half empty!"

Dad and the two children looked surprised. "What! Oh really?" The room was very quiet. Everyone was thinking.

"I think the cookie monster stole them!" said Dad. "I've heard that just before Christmas he sniffs and snoops around until he finds out where the cookies are hidden. I bet he got close to the closet and smelled your delicious cinnamon stars..."

"Exactly!" agreed little sister. "They were so good that he got the chest out again and ate a lot of the coconut macaroons."

"But the ones he liked best were the almond cookies!" admitted little brother.

"I see," said Mom. "And what does this cookie monster look like?" she asked.

"He has fuzzy hair with dark curls," answered Dad.

"And blue-and-white-striped arms," said little sister.

"But his stomach is green and red just like my sweatshirt!" added little brother.

"He sounds really scary!" said Mom. "I'm happy that I never saw him. I would have been scared to death!"

"You sure would have," the three of them nodded in agreement.

"So now what?" asked Mom. "I don't have time to bake any more cookies. But we certainly don't have enough for the holidays. I don't know what we should do."

"We could bake them," offered Dad. "You just have to tell us how. And then afterwards we'll guard them carefully so that the cookie monster doesn't get into them anymore! Isn't that right, kids?"

Little brother and little sister nodded together.

"And I'll draw you a picture of him," said little brother excitedly. "He's so scary that if you put his picture on the cookie jar, he'll be afraid of himself!"

Mom smiled as they all hugged her.

"No, I certainly don't have to be afraid of the cookie monster," laughed the little angel. "But seriously, have you thought of a special present yet?"

"Unfortunately not," answered the old rabbit. "The only things I can think of are too ordinary." They both thought a little more. Then the old rabbit added, "I did see a star once that was pretty special. It came out of the sea! Can you imagine that!

"Yes," said the little angel. "Because that little star once lived in the sky with us!"

And the little angel told the fourteenth story.

MOONCHILD, STAR OF THE SEA

A little star sat on a silver moonbeam and gazed down at the earth.

"What are those dark places?" the star asked the moon.

"That is the land where people live," she answered.

"What are those beautiful blue places?"

"That is the sea," said the moon. "We are good friends."

"Please tell me more about the sea," begged the little star.

"The sea is wonderful," said the moon. "Every night it glimmers with light from me and every day it sparkles in the sun," she continued. The little star couldn't hear enough about the sea.

One day the little star said, "Dear moon, I want to go and see the sea for myself. Can I?"

The moon smiled at him. "Of course. Once in their life, every star gets curious and wants to go. When you become a sea star, you'll get to live on earth until you have learned all that you can, and then you will return to the sky. It will be a wonderful adventure."

The moon looked fondly at the little star. "I will wait here for you," she said.

"But my light will always be there with you, even when you cannot see it."

So the star shut his eyes and a great beam of light shone out of the sky and into the night of the deep blue sea.

The star slept deeply for a long time. When he woke, he felt the stroke of the water on his arms. "Look, he's moving," whispered a voice near him.

"He's so beautiful," said another. And a new life began for the little star. He played with his new friends everyday and he learned a lot from the waves of the sea. He saw mussels, fish, algae, and coral. It was very exciting.

Each night the sea star made his way back to the cliff that rose up from the beach. He felt safe there, because he could see the light of the moon.

One day, the little star felt that he had learned all that he could learn here. He longed to see distant shores, far-off oceans, and unimaginable creatures.

So he left. He saw busy ports with huge boats and lots of people. He smelled beautiful flowers and heard music from unusual birds. He even swam with whales and dolphins.

Year after year, the little star continued his journey throughout the world. He saw children playing on the beach and once he even saw houses covered with snow. Just like the sea, the land was full of magic, and each day the sea star learned something new.

But one day, the little star grew tired. That was when he knew that he had learned all that he could.

So the star decided to return home. He went back to the sea and swam to his beloved cliff. It was so much fun to see all of his old friends again! He told them stories about his great adventure. Then is was time to go—on a beautiful autumn night, when the moon was full and his friends were all around...

The star shut his eyes and a great beam of light shone out of the sea and into the night of the deep, deep sky.

The star woke with the wind brushing his arms. He felt like he had slept deep and long.

The moon smiled at him. "Hello again, dear star," she said. "It's nice to have you back."

And far away on a lonely beach, a child found a beautiful star that had washed up on the sand. He picked it up and took it home.

And when Christmas came, the child hung it above the manger.

"So that's how it was," said the old rabbit. "I never would have thought of that. There really are a lot of curious things that happen between heaven and earth, aren't there?"

"Yes, there are," agreed the little angel. "So just help me think of one thing that might be alright for a present!" pleaded the little angel.

The old rabbit thought harder. "What about flowers?"

"Flowers? Not even snowmen with carrot noses found flowers outside in the snow!" said the little angel.

"That's right – no colorful flowers in winter," said the rabbit.

"But that's not exactly true. They are very rare, but I have seen some."

And the old rabbit told the fifteenth story.

THE CHRISTMAS FLOWER

Mr. Samuels loved perfect flower gardens. He had his garden divided into four exact rows. Mr. Samuels grew a spring, a summer, a fall, and a winter garden. From the last snowfall in winter all the way to autumn, his flowers bloomed exactly as he planned. Well, all except for his winter garden under the fir tree. It was completely empty. Nothing bloomed during the cold winter months.

The old gardener worked hard, day and night. He cleared away the grass, swept the sidewalk, weeded, and plucked everything in sight, until his garden looked perfect. Weeds were afraid of Mr. Samuels.

A little girl named Cecilia lived next door to him. She had the wildest garden anyone could imagine. It was a real jungle. Vines were the foundation of her house. Bamboo sprouts grew in every corner. Dandelions took over the grass. And ivy climbed everything—even the street light.

When Mr. Samuels stood on his ladder to trim his trees, he could see over the wall into his Cecilia's garden. "It's unbelievable how wild your garden looks," he shouted to Cecilia disgusted.

"It is, isn't it? I think so too!" she answered as she continued to play Tarzan with her friend.

The old man turned around angrily. He could really dislike her if she wasn't so sweet. She would help him in the garden sometimes. Yes, she was a little green fairy, she was. If only she weren't so in love with dandelion salad and poison ivy soup! he thought.

"Be careful that your jungle doesn't take over my house, too!" he yelled at Cecilia one day while he was picking apples. "How can you let that leafy stuff grow all over your walls?"

"Ivy is good for the house," Cecilia yelled from her tree house. "It protects the wall from the rain!"

"And you expect me to believe that!" grumbled Mr. Samuels. "Next you'll be telling me that in your magical garden, flowers bloom even in winter!"

Cecilia giggled. "You never know! There's something peculiar growing under my fir tree. It has long leaves with a bud. I don't know what it is. Maybe it's a Christmas flower!"

"It's nothing more than a weed, so pull it out!" yelled Mr. Samuels.

"Christmas flowers...yeah, right! When that happens, I'll let everything grow wild in my garden, too!"

"Oh, that would be great!" Cecilia said excitedly. Mr. Samuels just shook his head. Flowers in winter! This little girl has read too many fairytales!

Winter came and it was cold and dark. No more flowers. No more leaves. Nothing. Everything looked sad. The old gardener spent the whole day alone inside the house.

On Christmas Eve, just as Mr. Samuels was sitting down to eat dinner, he heard someone calling his name. "Mr. Samuels! Mr. Samuels! Come quick!" It was Cecilia's voice. "I have to show you something," she said, all excited. Cecilia led him into her garden. In the darkest corner, underneath the fir tree, a strange bud had bloomed.

It looked like a shining star in the night. Mr. Samuels was speechless.

"It's beautiful," he said when he was finally able to speak. "It's lucky you didn't pull it out…"

"Cecilia, what are you doing?" called her mother. "I'm coming," she called back. She took Mr. Samuels by the hand. "And you're coming with me. The Christmas flower is my present for you. We're going to plant it in your beautiful garden this spring. Merry Christmas, Mr. Samuels!"

The old gardener smiled and went with Cecilia into her house. It was the nicest Christmas he had had in a long time.

And since that day, the old gardener began to let everything grow freely in his garden. And he and Cecilia knew that he had the most beautiful garden in the whole world!

"Can you show me where Christmas roses grow?" asked the little angel. "Please!"

"Sure I can," said the old rabbit. "But this year the flowers are a bit late. They're still too small to pick."

"Oh, my stars!" said the little angel annoyed. "We can't seem to come up with anything! Just say something," suggested the little angel. "Tell me anything that comes into your mind".

While the old rabbit listened, he saw the messy raven's nest in the bare, leafless trees and said, "A raven!"

"What?" said the little angel, laughing at the old rabbit. "That's not a present—that's a story..."

And the little angel told the sixteenth story.

SNOW RAVENS

Three ravens were perched on a branch of an old tree.

It was the dead of winter, and freezing cold. The ravens pressed themselves feathers-to-feathers in a feeble attempt to keep warm.

"I'm so cold!" squawked the first raven, wrapping his wings tightly around his body.

"Oh, I hate the snow!" grumbled the second.

The third raven didn't say anything at all.

"White, white, nothing but white everywhere," croaked the first raven, dreaming of golden cornfields dotted with red poppies.

"It's so depressing," agreed the second, thinking of the sweet cherries he liked to eat in the summertime.

The third raven didn't say anything at all. Shyly, he peeked at the children and listened to their giggles as they stomped around in the field. He thought it might be fun to play with them.

"Brrrrrrr," whimpered the first raven.

"Oh, woe," whined the second one.

The third raven didn't say anything at all.

So there they sat. One hour passed. Then two hours. Then the whole afternoon drifted by. At that point a pile of snow plopped down on their heads from the branch above.

The first two ravens complained loudly.

The third raven just chuckled, imagining that the snow on his head was a crown.

Suddenly, the ravens heard shouting and cheering.

"How can those children be so loud!" said the first raven.

"So unbelievably loud!" agreed the second.

The third raven peeked curiously down to see what the children were doing.

How strange. The children were lying on their backs in the snow, waving their arms and legs as if they were wings. "Look at my snow angel!" they shouted, standing up to admire the figures they had made in the snow.

I would love to try that, thought the third raven.

The sun was setting by the time the children headed for home. The third raven stretched his damp limbs and flew off. Gently, he landed on the field.

He tried all sorts of things. He pressed his feathery belly into the snow, spread his wings, and wiggled his tail. He jumped up and down and spun in a circle. Impossible. His snow prints looked more like moles or elephants or kangaroos—anything but angels.

But the third raven didn't give up. He flapped his wings even harder, jumped higher in the air, spun in a circle, and each time he landed, he made even crazier shapes in the snow. At last he landed flat on his back with his wings spread far out to the sides. He couldn't get back up.

From the tree above him, he heard snickering. "Look down there," said the first raven.

"Looks like a bird swimming on his back," said the second raven.

They laughed for a long time.

The third raven felt a little embarrassed. Quietly, he lay there in the snow.

Finally the other two ravens flew down and helped him up.

The next morning the third raven sat by himself on the tree branch. Before long some children appeared. Happily they stomped around the field and began to play. Suddenly they noticed the brand-new teeny-tiny print in the snow. It was such a sweet little image—so delicate. There was no doubt—

"It must have been made by a real angel!" the children declared.

The raven felt very proud, so proud that he didn't even notice that it had begun to snow.

White flakes landed on his black feathers, and soon he was completely white.

Just then, one of the children saw the raven sitting in the tree.

"Look!" he cried. "It's the tiny angel!" The children stared in wonder.

Above them, the raven took a deep breath, threw back his head, and let out a loud long caw that echoed joyfully in the cold winter air.

"Too bad, the raven gave himself away," smiled the old rabbit.

"It didn't really matter," said the little angel. "The children were still really happy. You don't see a white raven everyday!"

"No, you don't. You don't hear great stories everyday either," said the little angel. "Come on. Time is running out. Can't you think of anything?"

"What about a gift certificate?" suggested the old rabbit. "That would make it easy."

"What's a gift certificate?" asked the little angel. "I've never heard of it."

"It's like a promise," explained the old rabbit. "A promise for something wonderful! And then when the time is right, you get the right present later. Like with Davy..."

And the rabbit told the seventeenth story.

MERRY CHRISTMAS, DAVY!

Christmas was coming. The woods were buried under a thick blanket of snow, but the Rabbit family was safe and warm inside its burrow. Father Rabbit asked the children, "What does Santa Claus like us to do?"

"He likes us to be good," said Davy.

"And to help one another," said Donny.

"And to share things!" added Daisy.

"And to be kind and loving," said big brother Dan.

"I see you've all been paying attention," said Father, smiling. "Good night."

The next day was really cold, so Davy and his toy rabbit Nicky stayed indoors. Davy saw a tiny bird hopping up and down, pecking the snow.

"Look, Nicky, he's trying to find something to eat," said Davy, "but he won't find anything. The snow is much too deep."

Davy remembered what Father had said last night. "Santa Claus likes us to help one another. I'll go and find some food for the birds." Davy found a big sack of corn and he scattered it under the old pine tree. But what about the deer, the wild pigs, and the squirrels? he thought. Their food is hidden under the snow, too! Davy carried hay, apples, carrots, and acorns to the old pine tree.

"Mother and Father will be so pleased with me for helping the animals. Santa Claus will be happy, too!"

Soon his family returned to the burrow.

"Hello, Davy," said Mother. Then she noticed that the larder door was open and saw the half-empty shelves. "Davy!" she cried. "Where is our food?"

"I...I... gave it to the hungry animals," Davy stammered.

"Are you crazy?" shouted Dan. "What are we going to eat all winter?"

Davy hadn't thought about that. He turned to his father. "You said we should help others, and share things, and love one another. We had so much, and the animals out there had nothing, so I ..." Davy's eye filled with tears.

"Wa-a-a-a!" wailed Daisy. "Davy has given our food away. Now we're going to starve!"

"Dinah hungry!" squeaked their baby sister.

And Donny muttered. "What a fool!"

"Don't say that," said Father. "Davy is right. We had a lot, and the other animals had very little, so we shared our food and everything will be okay."

"That's true," said Mother. "If we are careful, our food will last until spring. What's important is that we love and help each other now. "

Time flew by until Christmas. Everyone was careful not to waste any food. Sometimes Davy didn't even eat all of his share. He took the last few crumbs over to the pine tree and scattered them on the ground. He didn't want the animals to think he had forgotten them. Then it was Christmas Eve. The rabbits were decorating their Christmas tree when they heard a loud knock on the door. "Is it Santa Claus?" whispered Daisy.

Davy ran to the door and opened it. But when he opened it, he saw birds, deer, squirrels, and wild pigs standing outside.

One of the birds gave him a twig, laden with berries. "Thank you, Davy. We are grateful to you for helping us and we want to give you something too, but right now we don't have very much. Next summer we're going to show you where the sweetest berries grow," he said.

One of the deer gave Davy a small bundle of wheat. The squirrels had brought some mushrooms. And a wild pig dropped some carrots and an apple at Davy's feet. "Next summer we're going to show you where all the best food is."

"Merry Christmas, Davy!" cried all the animals. They slipped quietly back into the woods.

Davy was very happy. "Now I have enough apples and berries to bake a Christmas cake," Mother said.

Davy put a berry in Dinah's mouth. "Next summer you can have lots more. My friends will show us where all the nicest things grow."

"And we will have so much food that we will share it with the animals again. No one will be hungry next winter," said Mother. Then they hugged each other and said, "Merry Christmas, everyone. Merry Christmas, Davy!"

"Wow!" I like what Davy did," admitted the little angel. "I think it's cool when you like to share, because it's not always easy for everybody—even if they have a lot of stuff."

"You're right," said the old rabbit. "I bet angels know a lot about sharing, don't they?"

"Actually, yes," he nodded.

And the little angel told the eighteenth story.

A WINTER STORY

Once there was a man.

He owned a house, an ox, a cow, a donkey, and a herd of sheep.

The young boy that herded the sheep owned a small dog, a thin wool shepherd's cloak, a shepherd's stick, and a shepherd's lamp.

The ground was covered with snow. It was cold and the young shepherd was freezing.

"Can I warm myself in your home?" the young shepherd asked the old man.

"I can't share my warmth. The wood is too expensive," answered the old man. And he left the young shepherd standing in the cold.

The young shepherd saw a bright star in the sky. "I wonder what that could be?" he thought. He took his stick and his lamp and followed the star.

"I won't stay here without the shepherd," barked the dog.

"I won't stay here without the dog," baaed the sheep.

"I won't stay here without the sheep," brayed the donkey.

"I won't stay here without the donkey," mooed the cow.

"I won't stay here without the cow," bellowed the ox.

So they all followed the smell of the young shepherd.

As the old man sat in his warm house, he thought, "It's very quiet."

He called to the shepherd outside, but there was no answer.

The old man went to the stall to see why it was so quiet, but the stall was empty.

Then the old man saw the footprints. "The shepherd has left and stolen my animals!" he shouted angrily. "I'm going to get my animals back!" And the old man followed the footprints.

Not long after he left, it began to snow. The snowflakes fell thicker and thicker. The footprints were soon covered up by the snow and the old man was freezing.

He sank deeper and deeper into the snow. A storm came and he didn't know which way to go or what to do. The old man wanted to give up.

At that very moment, the snow stopped and the man saw a bright star in the sky. "I wonder what that could be?" he thought. He decided to follow the star.

The star glistened above a stall in the middle of an open field. Through a small window, the old man thought he could see the reflection of a shepherd's lamp.

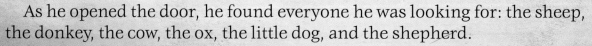

As he opened the door, he found everyone he was looking for: the sheep, the donkey, the cow, the ox, the little dog, and the shepherd.

They were all gathered around a manger.

A child lay inside the manger.

The small child smiled at the old man as if he had been expecting him.

"I've been rescued," the old man said. And he knelt down next to the shepherd in front of the manger.

The next morning, the old man, the shepherd, the sheep, the donkey, the cow, the ox, and the little dog headed home together.

The ground was covered in snow. It was cold.

"Come inside," the old man said to the shepherd. "I have more than enough wood to share the warmth!"

"Lovely," said the old rabbit. "Unfortunately, we still haven't come up with a present."

"I know," said the little angel. "I just can't think of anything, can you?"

"What about a doll?" suggested the old rabbit. "A doll is like a friend to play with and love."

"Yeah, but it's supposed to be a boy's present," said the little angel.

"Do you really think that only girls can play with dolls?" asked the old rabbit.

"Well, maybe not," said the little angel feeling a little embarrassed.

"I think you need to hear the story about Jonathan," the old rabbit decided.

And he told the nineteenth story.

A DOLL FOR JONATHAN

"Jonathan, what do you want for Christmas?" his mother asked during dinner one night.

"I want a doll," he answered excitedly.

"Really, a doll?" smiled his dad. "But you already have so many stuffed animals. Wouldn't you rather have a parking garage for your cars?"

"No," said Jonathan. "A doll."

"Jonathan, have you already written your letter to Santa?" his grandmother and grandfather asked him when they came to visit.

"Not yet!" answered Jonathan.

"You probably want a new sled," said grandfather. "Or a toolbox," interrupted grandmother.

"No. I want a doll," Jonathan said again.

The next morning in kindergarten, Jonathan drew a picture of a doll on a large sheet of paper. "Would you write something for me?" he asked his teacher. "Please write, 'This is what I want for Christmas! Sincerely yours, Jonathan.'"

"Hey, did you hear that?" yelled Mark, who was sitting next to the teacher's desk. "Jonathan wants a doll! A doll!"

The other children in the class laughed too... all of them except Lisa.

Jonathan carefully rolled up his picture to take it home.

After school Lisa came upstairs to Jonathan's house to play. They built a city out of building blocks, towels, and boxes.

Jonathan built a house. "If I had a doll, she could live here," he said.

Lisa built a street for her cars to drive on. "If I had a garage, I could park my cars there," she said.

After dinner, Jonathan went to his window and left his picture outside on the windowsill.

Finally, Christmas morning arrived. Jonathan was so excited. He ran to the tree. There were lots of presents wrapped in colorful paper with silver and gold ribbon. There was also a red sled.
But, where was the doll? It wasn't there.

Santa had brought Jonathan a sled, a parking garage with an elevator, a tool chest, and a new jacket, but no doll.

While the grown-ups were eating cake, Jonathan took his parking garage and left the room. His mother thought that he was going to carry it to his room. But instead, he slipped down the stairs to Lisa's house and knocked on her door.

When Lisa opened the door, she held a wonderful doll in her arms.

"I got a garage," smiled Jonathan. "Would you like to have it?"

"I got another doll," laughed Lisa. "Would you like to have her?"

They exchanged their presents.

"I wonder how that happened?" asked Jonathan.

"Hmm," said Lisa. "Maybe Santa got our letters mixed up."

"Oh well, it really doesn't matter. The important thing is that we both got what we really wanted!"

Overjoyed, Jonathan ran home to his parents.

"Look what Santa brought me!" he said.

He hugged his doll and stroked her hair. "You wait," he whispered.

"I'm going to be the best dad in the whole world!"

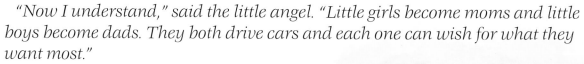

"Now I understand," said the little angel. "Little girls become moms and little boys become dads. They both drive cars and each one can wish for what they want most."

"Exactly," nodded the old rabbit.

"But there are some children who wish for way too many things," commented the little angel. "You can't imagine how long some of the lists are that come to us. When I just think about Timothy's list!" The little angel laughed.

The old rabbit was nosey and asked, "Why, what was so special about it?"

And the little angel told the twentieth story.

SANTA'S GIFT

Humphrey was still in bed when Timothy knocked on his door.

"Wake up! I got a letter. You have to read it to me," he shouted loud enough to wake Humphrey.

What? thought Humphrey. A letter for Timothy? Humphrey was surprised. Timothy never shared his toys so he didn't have any friends. Except for Humphrey. Humphrey loved everybody. And everybody loved him. The letter was from Santa Claus!

> *Dear Timothy,*
> *I received your Christmas wish list, but there is a problem. I can't find anything big enough or fun enough to keep you happy for a whole year.*
> *Love,*
> *Santa Claus*

Timothy began to cry, "No, no, no! I want to have a new toy. I have to! Please help me write a letter to Santa."

So Humphrey helped him.

> *Dear Santa Claus,*
> *Please, please, please bring me a present. It doesn't matter what it is, I promise I'll play with it until next Christmas.*
> *Yours,*
> *Timothy*

The next morning Timothy ran to Humphrey's with a new letter.

> *Dear Timothy,*
> *I found the best present of all for you. You will be surprised!*
> *Yours,*
> *Santa Claus*

Timothy was excited about the good news!

Finally, Christmas morning arrived. Timothy raced to the Christmas tree. Wow! There were presents everywhere. But when he looked at the tags, there were a lot of names he didn't know. "Oh, no!" cried Timothy. "Santa delivered these presents to the wrong house. Somebody else has my new toy!"

Humphrey came in to see what was wrong. Between sobs, Timothy explained the mix-up. Humphrey just couldn't believe it. He'd never heard of Santa Claus making a mistake.

Then Humphrey saw a note attached to the Christmas tree.

Dear Timothy,
The thing I enjoy most throughout the year is the joy of giving.
So this is the gift I give to you. For Christmas, you get to hand out
some of my presents. Have fun!
Yours,
Santa Claus

"This is a wonderful present," said Humphrey. "You should get started."

"I can't," whined Timothy. "Nobody will play with me so I don't know where any of them live!"

Humphrey thought about it. "I think I can help you…"

Not long after that, Humphrey hung a sign up in the middle of town. A little time later there was a knock at Timothy's door. Lots of kids were there shouting "Merry Christmas!"

"Welcome to Timothy's Christmas party," said Humphrey. "Come inside."

He picked up some of the packages and started calling out the names. The kids cheered with excitement. As Timothy saw their faces light up, he began to feel different.

"Stop, Humphrey. Wait!" called Timothy. "This is MY gift from Santa. I'M suppose to hand out the presents!"

The children played together and had a great celebration. Eventually it was time to go home.

"Thank you, Timothy!" said the last guests as they were leaving. "It was really fun! Would you like to play with us tomorrow?"

Timothy's face glowed. "Of course I would. I'd love to!"

Timothy waved goodbye to his new friends.

Late in the evening there was another knock at Timothy's door.

No one was there, but he found a letter.

Dear Timothy,
You did a great job! I'm very proud of you…
So proud that I have decided to reward you by
making you an official Santa's Helper! Congratulations!
Your friend,
Santa Claus

P. S. I look forward to visiting you next year!

"That was a wonderful idea that Santa Claus had," said the old rabbit.
"Timothy got new friends. That's a present that will last a long time!"
"You're right and Timothy never sent any more monster-wish lists," said the angel.
"Your story reminds me of something that happened a long time ago in the city near us," said the rabbit. "The teddy bears prepared an unforgettable Christmas celebration for all the people."
"The teddy bears? How did they do that?" wondered the little angel.
And the old rabbit told the twenty-first story.

THE BEARS' CHRISTMAS SURPRISE

It was Christmas Eve. A bear with a red bow tie sat forgotten on the bookshelf. He had been there for years. Hours of play and then neglect had made his fur dull and shaggy. But the corner of his eyes still held the glow from the first time he was held in a child's arms.

He was the first bear to disappear. When he reached the abandoned shed, he waited. One by one, from everywhere around the town, the other bears slipped away. They tiptoed out of children's rooms, squeezed out of toy chests, and climbed down from shop window displays. One after another they came—fleecy bears with friendly faces, elegant bears, and delicate bears, bears with frizzy fur and even velvet ones. There was also a tiny one in an angel costume. Just as they were all assembled, the bells in the church tower struck midnight. Satisfied that not a single bear was missing, the little bear in the red bow tie nodded. That was the sign.

The bears rushed outside and spread throughout the town eager to begin their work. Silently they climbed over fences and balconies, slid down chimneys and crawled through cat flaps. They headed straight for the presents that were wrapped and ready for Christmas morning. Swiftly the bears untied every bow. They slipped off the wrapping paper and removed each gift. Then they wrote little notes in their squiggly bear writing, put them into the boxes, and wrapped them up again.

Just before dawn, when the bears had finished their surprise, they returned to their places in children's rooms, toy chests, and shop windows.

The bears' prank caused a perfect mess. Children cried when they opened their presents to find empty boxes. The parents saw the notes and ran to their neighbors for help, but in each house it was the same story. All the presents were gone and no one knew what had happened.

The sad people sat in their homes and read the mysterious messages over and over again. Each time they read them their hearts beat more quickly and their disappointment melted away:

"This package is as empty as my arms."

"My heart remembers when you ran to me with joy."

"I am longing for a cheerful visit."

"Do you remember me? I think of you often."

And suddenly they thought of all the lonely people in the city. They realized it must be awful to be forgotten and all alone on Christmas Day.

Quickly, they put on their warmest clothes and left. They visited the grandmother in the nursing home, the aunt who sat alone by the window, and the man who missed his own family terribly. Not a single person in the city was overlooked.

And in each home they visited, they found gifts. No one knew how they had gotten there. Soon laughter and music rang from brightly lit windows. Over and over the same phrase was heard, "Merry Christmas!"

The next night, the bears who slept alone—those that were left behind on shelves, in toy boxes, or in the shops—these bears were called back to the abandoned shed. To their surprise, they found a great tree, hung with glowing candles. Under its arching branches lay a pile of presents, one for each bear. And for that long night, the bears forgot their loneliness and played until morning.

"The teddy bears had a wonderful idea for a present," whispered the little angel. "I guess I'm just too small and silly, because I can't come up with anything."

"Don't worry," the old rabbit said trying to comfort the little angel. "We'll find something that will be perfect. Besides, you're not silly. Just think about the example that Willard set. Look at him now."

"Which one is Willard?" asked the little angel.

"The little fir tree there," answered the old rabbit. "He is also something special."

And the old rabbit told the twenty-second story...

WILLARD, THE LITTLE CHRISTMAS TREE

Once there was a very small fir tree named Willard. He grew at the edge of the forest. The birds didn't build their nests there. The squirrels didn't climb up to eat their nuts and acorns there. And none of the children played there. Willard hated being small. He felt as if nobody took him seriously. Some day I'll show them, thought Willard. But he didn't know how.

One day two hares came over the meadow to the edge of the forest. "Hey, take a look at that!" said one of them, pointing to Willard. "We can use him for jumping practice. He's just the right size." The hare got a running start and took a great leap, right over Willard. The second hare did the same.

Willard was green with anger. But no matter how high he stretched, he couldn't even reach the hair on their bellies with his needles. Just you wait, he thought. Someday I'll show you. He just didn't know how.

Another time, a hedgehog came by. She was in a terrible mood. She'd been rummaging through the nearby trash, and now her spines were all messy. She was covered with potato peelings, bread crusts, and even a salami wrapper!

When she saw Willard, she exclaimed, "Oh, my, he's just the right size!" And before he could pull back his needles, the hedgehog scooted in among his branches and scraped off all the muck.

Willard trembled with fury. Just you wait! he thought. Someday I'll show all of you! But he still didn't know how.

Winter came and so did the snow. Willard stood mournfully at the edge of the meadow. Every once in a while he would shake the snow from his branches so he wouldn't completely disappear in a drift.

One bright morning a man and his son approached Willard. "This one here? It's so small," said the man.

"Not for me. For me it's just the right size," replied the little boy.

The man thought about it. "You're right. It's beautiful. And it is exactly your size. But it would be a shame to cut it down when it's still so young. What if we were to decorate him right here? Then it could be your Christmas tree every year."

"Oh yes!" said the boy happily. "It'll grow and I will grow. So it'll always be perfect for me!"

That very afternoon the little boy came back to the forest with his parents. They pulled a sled with a big box on it. Inside the box were beautiful red and blue glass balls to hang on Willard's branches. He was careful not to drop a single ball. There wasn't enough room for all the balls, so the little boy set the rest in a ring around Willard's base.

Finally, the little boy fastened a gold star on the top. The star was quite heavy, but Willard was so proud that he didn't bend a bit.

"Wonderful," said the father.

"It's the most beautiful Christmas tree I've ever seen," said the little boy.

Willard was very happy. He was a Christmas tree.

And it didn't matter if he was big or small, because a Christmas tree is the best tree of all!

The next day, all the animals came to see Willard. They were in awe of his beauty. Willard knew that he had finally shown them that he was indeed just the right size—for something truly special.

Every year at Christmas time, the little boy came back. Every year the little boy and Willard grew a little bigger, but no matter how tall the little boy grew—Willard was just the right size!

"Can we take a closer look at Willard?" asked the little angel.

"Of course!" answered the old rabbit as he led the way through the deep snow.

"Soon Willard will be the most beautiful Christmas tree of all." The old rabbit blew the snow from Willard's branches. "And you my little friend will become a real Christmas angel!"

"Do you really think so?" asked the little angel. "It would make me so happy!"

"Do you know what would make me happy?" asked the old rabbit.

"No. What?" answered the little angel.

"I would like you to tell Willard and me the story of the first Christmas!"

"No problem!"

And the little angel told the twenty-third story.

SILENT NIGHT

A long, long time ago, a man and a woman were traveling to a distant city. Their names were Mary and Joseph. Mary was going to have a child and couldn't walk very far, so she rode on a donkey.

In the beginning, the donkey was stubborn and cried, "Hee-haw! Hee-haw!" Both the baggage and Mary were too much of a load for him.

But Joseph stroked the donkey and begged, "Please help us. The child that Mary carries is the son of God." This calmed the donkey and he allowed Mary to climb on. Their journey lasted many days.

"Oh, Joseph, I can't go any farther!" complained Mary one morning. She sat down on a rock and began to cry.
Joseph comforted her. "Just a little farther, Mary. Very soon we will reach Bethlehem. When we get there, we will look for a nice room in an inn. Tonight you will be able to sleep in a soft, comfortable bed!"

Mary stood up and began to walk farther.

But when they reached Bethlehem, the entire city was full of people. No one had a bed for the tired travelers. Even the last innkeeper on the edge of the city said, "I'm sorry, but there are no more rooms available." Sadly, Mary and Joseph continued through the city gates and left the noisy, over-filled city behind them. In the silence outside the gates, Joseph heard an ox. He turned around wondering where the sound had come from.

"Maybe there is a stall close by where we could spend the night," he said. It wasn't long before they had found one. It had a solid roof. There was hay to sleep on and a place to build a fire. A brown ox stood in one corner.

"Thank you for leading us here," smiled Joseph. "We would like to stay with you tonight." Joseph helped Mary down from the donkey and carried her inside. He laid her down in soft hay and covered her with his warm coat. She was very tired and closed her eyes.

Joseph gave the animals some food and water. He put out the light from the lantern and lay down in the hay. But during the night, a bright light woke him. Half asleep, he rubbed his eyes. Mary was on her knees beside a small manger. Something tiny and delicate moved around on the hay.

"Our child!" whispered Joseph. "Oh Mary, I don't believe it. God's child came into the world in an old stall!"

"It doesn't matter," smiled Mary. "It is perfect like this. Look how beautifully the light shines around him! We will call him Jesus..."

Just then, there was a soft knock at the door. "Who could that be?"

Hesitantly, Joseph unbolted the door. Shepherds stood outside with their sheep. "Can we please come in and see God's child?" begged the youngest shepherd.

"How did you know that God's child was born here?" wondered Joseph.

"God sent an angel to us in the fields," explained the young shepherd. "And the bright star in the sky showed us the way!"

It was true. An amazing star shone above the stall as a sign. "Please come in," said Joseph. The shepherds squeezed themselves into the small stall. They greeted Mary and presented simple gifts: bread, salt, a bottle of milk, and a wool blanket for the baby. The shepherds knelt down in front of the manger. It was very quiet. The youngest shepherd took his flute out of his bag and played a song for the baby Jesus. The song was about a silent night when a miracle occurred.

"I can listen to this story forever," said the old rabbit. "It is so beautiful."

Little Willard wiggled his snowy branches in agreement.

"Yes, it was beautiful, but it reminded me that I still haven't accomplished my task," sniffed the little angel. "Christmas is here and I haven't found a present. Instead of looking for something special, I wasted my time telling you useless stories."

"That's not true," said the old rabbit. "Stories are never useless. Quite the contrary, stories are wonderful. Telling stories means taking time. Telling stories means sharing something interesting. Telling stories means that you love someone. I think there is no better present in the whole world than telling a story…"

The little angel and the old rabbit stared at each other.

"Oh my stars!" stuttered the little angel. "That means it was, it was..."

"...The gift of gifts," whispered the old rabbit.

"Hallelujah again!" cheered the angel and tossed his cap into the air. "Yippeee! We have a gift, the best gift of all!"

The little angel and the old rabbit hopped and danced around Willard. Suddenly the two of them fell down in the snow laughing. "Oh, isn't this wonderful!" sighed the little angel happily. "Just imagine how big their eyes will get when I get there with my gift! But wait a minute, you can't see it!"

"That's the beauty of it," laughed the old rabbit. "The stories themselves are invisible, but they are hidden in all of us around the world! But I have an idea. You should write down all of the stories that we have told. Then they can be read and shared however someone chooses."

"We could also paint pictures that go with the stories," added the little angel.

"And make a big book out of them. Then, the book could be the present. And every time someone takes time to read from it, it becomes another present!"

"Yeah, and above everything else, it never stops making people happy," said the old rabbit. "You have really found something special. You are a real Christmas Angel—just like Willard and I told you. That's cool!"

The little angel laughed and hugged the old rabbit so tightly that he could barely breathe. "Thank you for everything!" he added. "You are really above-the-clouds-top-class! I better hurry so that I get my gift back on time!"

He looked down at himself. "Oh, stars! I have to change clothes before I can tell my stories to all the children in the sky. Goodbye, Willard!" He shook the longest branch of the little fir tree.

"We wish you all the best!" called the old rabbit as the little angel was already on his way. "Are we going to see you again?"

"Of course," the little angel called back as he pulled his cap down tight over his ears. "I'll come back and read you something. Even though you already know the stories."

"You're right, but you can't hear really good stories often enough," smiled the old rabbit and Willard wiggled his branches in agreement.

"MERRY CHRISTMAS!"

SOURCES

Idea, concept, cover story, original title
DER ENGEL MIT DER BOMMELMÜTZE and
connecting stories 1–24: by Brigitte Weninger
Cover illustration, endpapers and vignettes for
titlepage and connecting stories by Miriam Monnier
Originally published by Neugebauer Verlag, 2002

1
Original title: HÄSCHEN WEISSOHR UND
DIE RÜBE
A traditional folktale, retold by Brigitte Weninger
Illustrator: Birte Müller

2
Original title: LUMINA (picture book)
Author: Brigitte Weninger
Illustrator: Julie Litty
Originally published by Neugebauer Verlag, 1997
ISBN: 3-85195-565-X

3
Original title: LANGEWEILE FÜR ANFÄNGER
Author: Linard Bardill
Illustrator: Miriam Monnier

4
Original title: DAS STERNENGEHEIMNIS
Author: Karl Rühmann
Illustrator: Mirko Rathke

5
Original title: MARTIN, DER SCHUSTER
Author: Leo Tolstoy, retold by Brigitte Weninger
Illustrator: Mirko Rathke

6
Original title: SANKT NIKOLAUS KOMMT
(picture book)
Author: Konrad Richter, retold by Brigitte Weninger
Illustrator: Jochen Stuhrmann
Originally published by Nord-Süd Verlag, 1985
ISBN: 3-314-00241-6

7
Original title: LUFTPOST FÜR DEN
WEIHNACHTSMANN (picture book)
Author: Brigitte Weninger
Illustrator: Anne Möller
Originally published by Neugebauer Verlag, 2000
ISBN: 3-85195-677-X

8
Original title:: SERAFIN SCHUTZENGEL
Author: Karl Rühmann
Illustrator: Mirko Rathke

9
Original title: DAS LEBKUCHENMÄNNCHEN
A traditional folktale, retold by Brigitte Weninger
Illustrator: Birte Müller

10
Original title: ANNAS WUNSCH
Author: Bruno Hächler
Illustrator: Nina Spranger

11
Original title: LIEBER SCHNEEMANN, WOHIN
WILLST DU? (picture book)
Author: Gerda Marie Scheidl
Illustrator: Elena Schern
Originally published by Nord-Süd Verlag, 1988
ISBN: 3-314-00325-0

12
Original title: PFANNKUCHEN FÜR DIE ENGEL
Author: Géraldine Elschner
Illustrator: Alexandra Junge

13
Original title: DAS PLÄTZCHENMONSTER
Author: Karl Rühmann
Illustrator: Sonja Bougajeva

14
Original title: STERNENKIND (picture book)
Author: Géraldine Elschner
Illustrator: Lieselotte Schwarz
Originally published by Neugebauer Verlag, 2002
ISBN: 3-85195-690-7

15
Original title: DIE CHRISTROSE
Author: Géraldine Elschner
Illustrator: Sonja Bougajeva

16
Original title: DER SCHNEERABE (picture book)
Author: Bruno Hächler
Illustrator: Birte Müller
Originally published by Neugebauer Verlag, 2002
ISBN: 3-85195-699-0

17
Original title: FRÖHLICHE WEIHNACHTEN,
PAULI! (picture book)
Author: Brigitte Weninger
Illustrator: Eve Tharlet
Originally published by Neugebauer Verlag, 1998
ISBN: 3-85195-588-9

18
Original title: EINE WINTERGESCHICHTE
(picture book)
Author: Max Bolliger
Illustrator: Alexandra Junge
Originally published by Nord-Süd Verlag, 1993
ISBN 3-314-00633-3

19
Original title: EINE PUPPE FÜR JONAS
Author: Brigitte Weninger
Illustrator: Nina Spranger

20
Original title: DAS SCHÖNSTE
WEIHNACHTSGESCHENK (picture book)
Author: Charise Neugebauer
Illustrator: Barbara Nascimbeni
Originally published by Neugebauer Verlag, 1999
ISBN: 3-85195-607-9

21
Original title: DAS GEHEIMNIS DER BÄREN
(picture book)
Author: Bruno Hächler
Illustrator: Angela Kehlenbeck
Originally published by Neugebauer Verlag, 2000
ISBN: 3-85195-648-6

22
Original title: WILLIBALD, DER
WEIHNACHTSBAUM (picture book)
Author: Karl Rühmann
Illustrator: Anne Möller
Originally published by Neugebauer Verlag, 2002
ISBN: 3-85195-700-8

23
Original title: STILLE NACHT
Author: Brigitte Weninger
Illustrator: Nina Spranger

24
Original title: DER 24. TAG
Author: Brigitte Weninger
Illustrator: Miriam Monnier